PENLIT PUBLISHING

THE CHRISTMAS PICKLE

ALDOUS BUNTING

Printed in the United States of America

First Printed Edition 2018
ISBN 978-1-7321263-9-8

PenLit Publishing
PO Box 2823
9009 SE Adams St
Clackamas, OR 97015

www.penlit.com

A very Merry Christmas to you all!

Christmas is a wonderful time of year where families all over the world celebrate with their favorite traditions.

One of these is the tradition of the Christmas pickle. A small pickle-shaped ornament is hidden on the tree and on Christmas morning the first person to find it receives a special gift.

It's an important job but for one Christmas pickle, it always caused a bit of a problem.

He wanted nothing more than to meet his hero, the big man himself, Santa Claus. Every year he would wait patiently hoping Santa would find him, but he was always too well hidden at the back of the tree.

He couldn't stand the thought of going another year without seeing Santa. He decided this year would be different.

"If Santa can't find me," he thought, "I'll go to him!" His plan was perfect. He would wait until everyone had gone to sleep on Christmas Eve. Then when the house was quiet, the Christmas Pickle would make his way to the front of the tree.

That night when the house fell quiet and the sounds of celebration could no longer be heard, the Christmas pickle prepared to make his journey to the front of the tree.

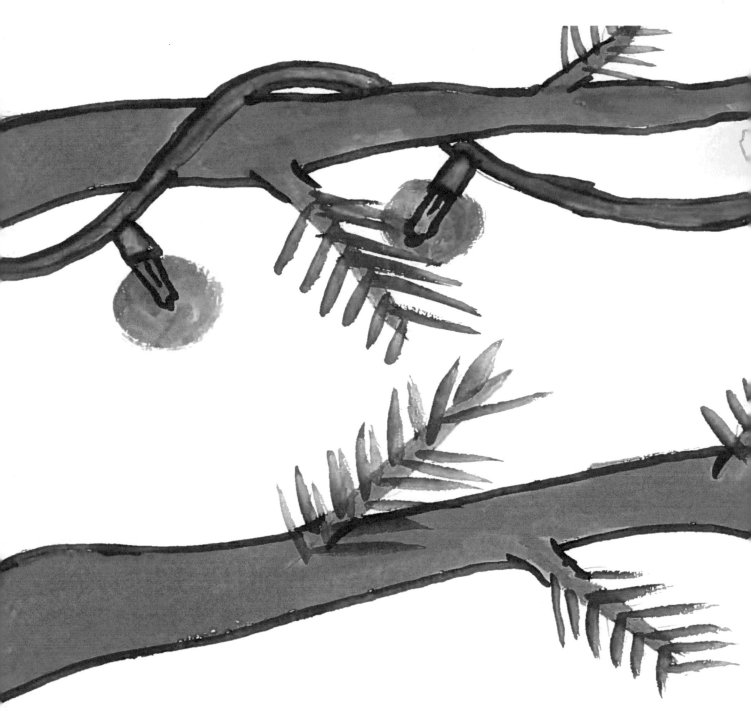

"Alright, the time is now," he thought. He looked at the branches and realized he had a small problem.
"I don't have any legs or arms. How am I going to get to the front of the tree?" He began to worry. Would his journey be over before it even began?

It was then that he looked up and noticed the hook he was hanging from. "I might be able to use my hook to swing to the front of the tree."

He began to move back and forth, building up his momentum and then he jumped. He sailed through the air and caught the next branch with his hook. "This just might work," he thought.

He was making excellent progress swinging from branch to branch. He made his way through the tree and soon enough he was getting close to the front. He could see the glass of milk and plate of cookies left out on the table for Santa. He could see the corner of the fireplace mantle where Santa would make his grand entrance.

"I'm almost there, just a few more branches." He sailed through the air as he made his final leap. His hook snagged the last branch and then he heard a loud snap!

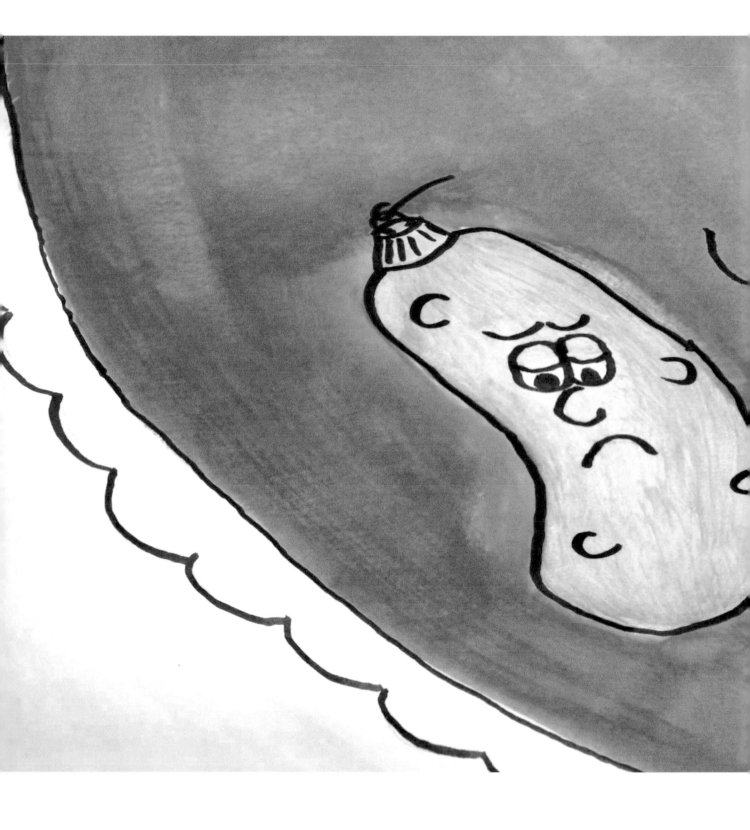

He looked up to see that the hook had broken from all
the swinging.

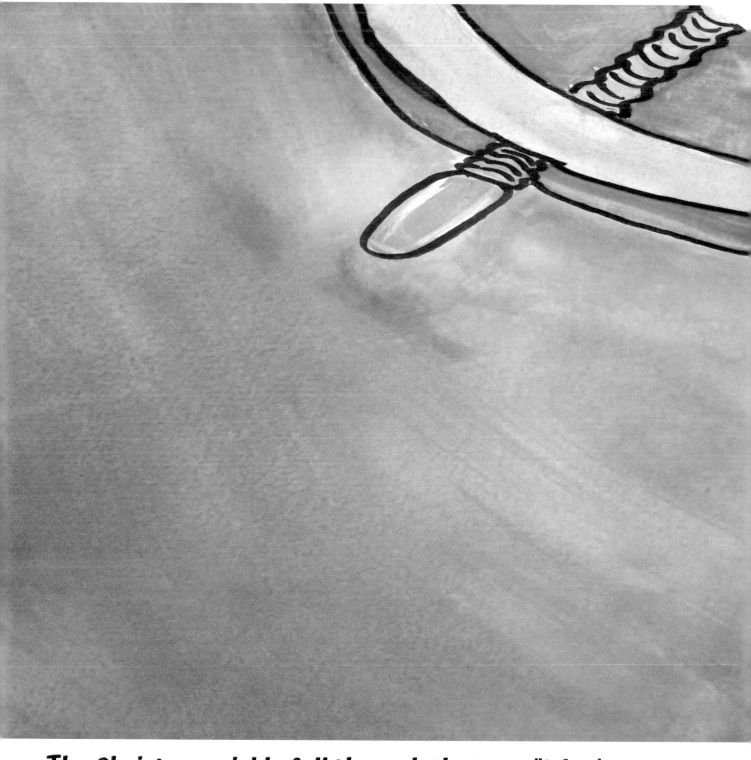

The Christmas pickle fell through the tree. "I don't have any arms!" he yelled unable to catch himself. He tumbled out of the tree, rolled down the tree skirt and landed with a soft thud on the carpet.

He looked up at the glowing lights of the tree standing above him. "This was a terrible idea," he thought. "I should have just stayed in my spot at the back of the tree. Why would Santa want to meet a silly old Christmas pickle anyway?"

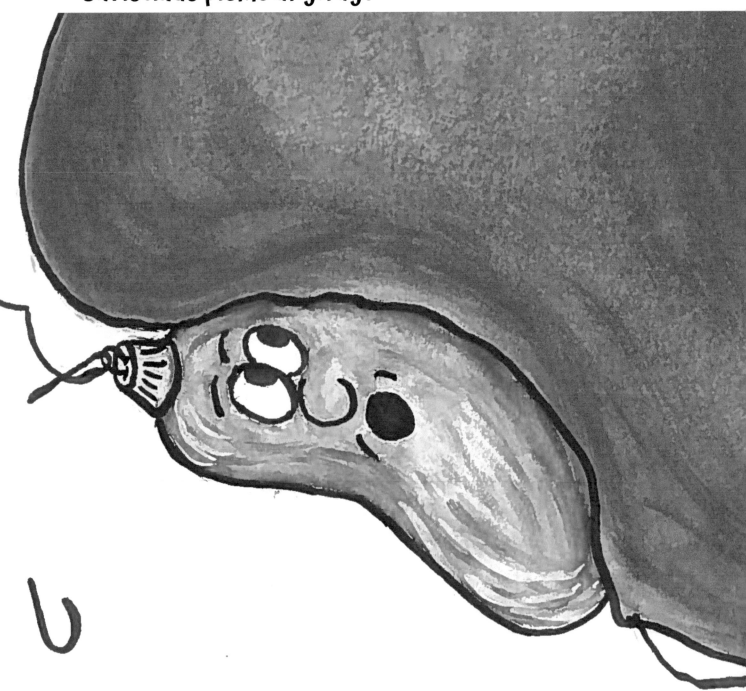

Then he heard it. That familiar sound that he knew so well. Sleigh bells ringing in the distance. They grew louder and then he heard the thud of reindeer hooves on the roof. Footsteps soon followed. "He's here, Santa is here! What if he's mad that I left my spot? I better hide." The Christmas pickle rolled to the side and tucked himself under the tree skirt.

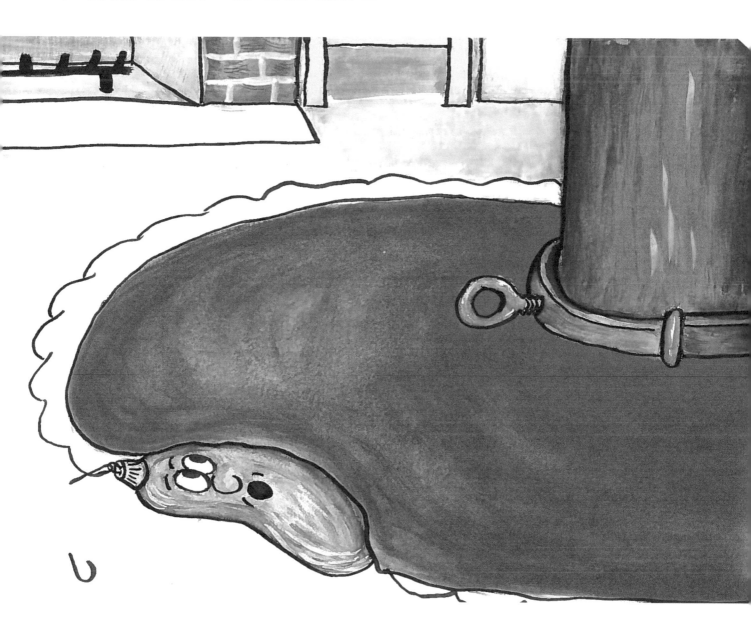

The fireplace crackled with the sound of dust falling from the chimney, and then with a whoosh, a thick cloud of soot exploded forth from the fireplace opening. The Christmas pickle watched as two shiny black boots stepped through the cloud and into the living room. It was really him, it was Santa Claus.

Santa walked softly over to the milk and cookies left for him. He took a bite of a cookie and washed it down with a big gulp of milk. He turned to admire the tree and noticed something was out of place.

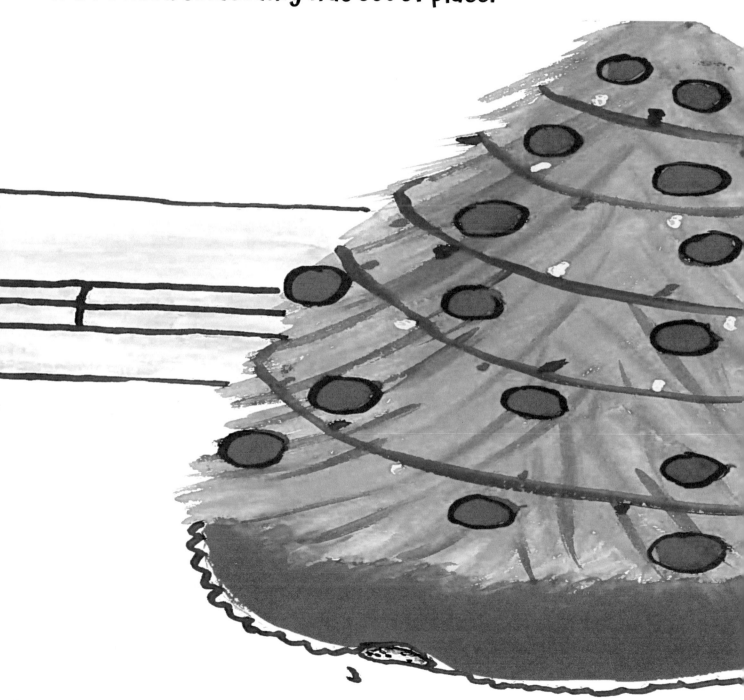

"What are you doing down there, friend?" Santa wondered aloud.

He bent over and picked up the Christmas pickle in his mitten-covered hand. "Why aren't you in your hiding spot at the back of the tree?" he asked.

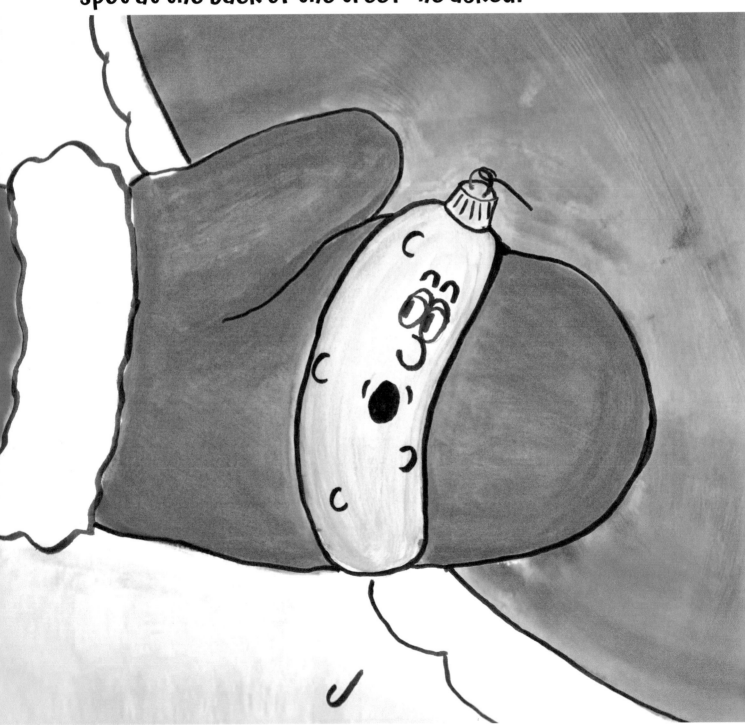

"I'm so sorry, Santa," the pickle said. "It's just that I'm your biggest fan and I've always wanted to meet you. I thought that I could come to the front of the tree and get back to my hiding spot before morning."

"Then my hook broke and I fell." Santa paused for a moment and then he smiled.

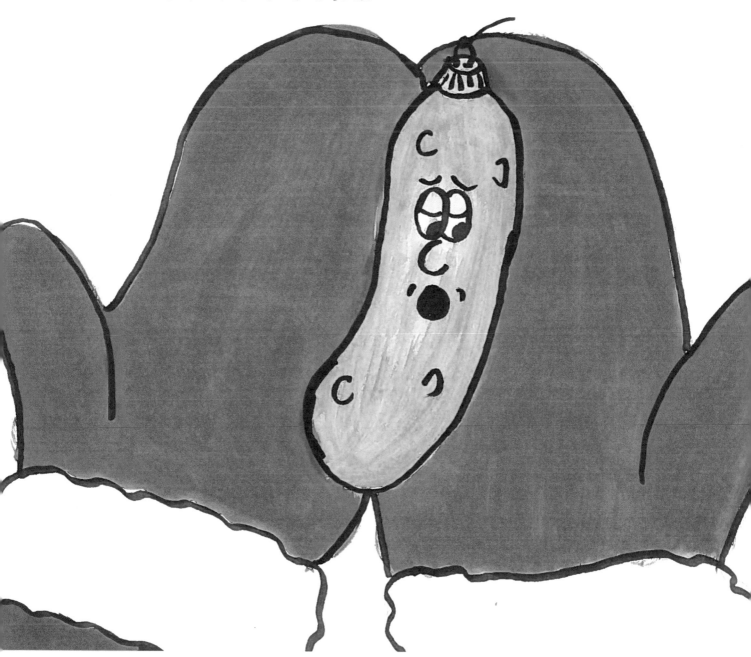

"Well, how about that? I'll have you know, I'm *your* biggest fan!" he said. The Christmas pickle couldn't believe what he was hearing.

"You know who I am?" the pickle asked surprised.

"Of course I do," said Santa. "The Christmas pickle is an important job and one of my favorite traditions. Just because I don't see you doesn't mean I don't know you're there."

Santa pulled out a shiny new hook from his pocket.

"Now let's get you back to your hiding spot."

Santa attached the new hook to the Christmas pickle and placed him back on the tree.

He placed the presents around the base of the tree and walked back over to the fireplace.

"Merry Christmas, friend," he said, and then he disappeared up the chimney.

The Christmas pickle hung there in his hiding spot, his heart full of happiness. As the sound of Santa's sleigh bells faded into the distance he smiled, what a great night it had been. He closed his eyes to get some sleep. He knew Christmas morning would be here soon and he had an important job to do.

As he dozed off, he thought to himself, sometimes all we have to do to make wonderful things happen is take the first leap.